BRINGING BACK THE

Lesser Long-Nosed Bat

Ruth Daly

Crabtree Publishing Company
www.crabtreebooks.com

CRABTREE
PUBLISHING COMPANY
WWW.CRABTREEBOOKS.COM

Author: Ruth Daly

Series Research and Development: Reagan Miller

Picture Manager: Sophie Mortimer

Design Manager: Keith Davis

Editorial Director: Lindsey Lowe

Children's Publisher: Anne O'Daly

Editor: Ellen Rodger

Proofreader: Wendy Scavuzzo

Cover design: Margaret Amy Salter

**Production coordinator and
    Prepress technician:** Margaret Amy Salter

Print coordinator: Katherine Berti

Produced for Crabtree Publishing Company
by Brown Bear Books

Photographs
(t=top, b= bottom, l=left, r=right, c=center)

Front Cover: All images from Shutterstock

Interior: Alamy: Phil Degginger 15t, Blaine Harrington III 22, Ronald Karpilo 17; Dreamstime: Steve Byland 21; iStock: Birdimages 10, cameralenta 9t, ChuckSchug Photography 13t Dr Ferry 14, Freder 8 Lindsay Lou 25b, mofles 12; IUCN: Bat Specialst Group 22cr; Public Domain: Enwebb 26, Faguilal 18, Mike Weston 6; Science Photo Library: Merlin D. Tuttle 20, 24; Shutterstock: Betancourt 19b, Bildagentur Zoonar GmbH 28, Johnny Coate 5, Danita Delmont 1, 4 7, FCHM 9b, FrameStockFootage 29, icolourful 25t, Tome Roche 16; UCSB.edu: 19t; U.S. Fish and Wildlife Service: 27t, 27b, Range News 13b.

All other photography and artwork Brown Bear Books.

Brown Bear Books has made every attempt to contact the copyright holder. If you have any information please contact licensing@ brownbearbooks.co.uk

Library and Archives Canada Cataloguing in Publication

Title: Bringing back the lesser long-nosed bat / Ruth Daly.
Names: Daly, Ruth, 1962- author.
Series: Animals back from the brink.
Description: Series statement: Animals back from the brink |
   Includes index.
Identifiers: Canadiana (print) 20190128224 |
   Canadiana (ebook) 20190128232 |
   ISBN 9780778763130 (hardcover) |
   ISBN 9780778763253 (softcover) |
   ISBN 9781427123336 (HTML)
Subjects: LCSH: Leptonycteris—Juvenile literature. |
   LCSH: Leptonycteris—Conservation—Juvenile literature. |
   LCSH: Bats—Juvenile literature. | LCSH: Bats—Conservation—
   Juvenile literature. | LCSH: Endangered species—Juvenile literature. |
   LCSH: Wildlife recovery—Juvenile literature.
Classification: LCC QL737.C57 D35 2019 | DDC j333.95/94516—dc23

Library of Congress Cataloging-in-Publication Data

Names: Daly, Ruth, 1962- author.
Title: Bringing back the lesser long-nosed bat / Ruth Daly.
Description: New York, New York : Crabtree Publishing Company,
   [2020] | Series: Animals back from the brink | Includes index.
Identifiers: LCCN 2019023702 (print) | LCCN 2019023703 (ebook) |
   ISBN 9780778763130 (hardcover) |
   ISBN 9780778763253 (paperback) |
   ISBN 9781427123336 (ebook)
Subjects: LCSH: Leptonycteris--Conservation--Juvenile literature.
Classification: LCC QL737.C57 D35 2020 (print) |
   LCC QL737.C57 (ebook) | DDC 599.4--dc23
LC record available at https://lccn.loc.gov/2019023702
LC ebook record available at https://lccn.loc.gov/2019023703

Crabtree Publishing Company

www.crabtreebooks.com   1-800-387-7650

Printed in the U.S.A./082019/CG20190712

**Published in Canada
Crabtree Publishing**
616 Welland Ave.
St. Catharines, Ontario
L2M 5V6

**Published in the United States
Crabtree Publishing**
PMB 59051
350 Fifth Avenue, 59th Floor
New York, New York 10118

**Published in the United Kingdom
Crabtree Publishing**
Maritime House
Basin Road North, Hove
BN41 1WR

**Published in Australia
Crabtree Publishing**
Unit 3–5 Currumbin Court
Capalaba
QLD 4157

Contents

Find videos and extra material online at **crabtreeplus.com** to learn more about the conservation of animals and ecosystems. See page 30 in this book for the access code to this material.

The Battle for Survival

The lesser long-nosed bat is a small, furry mammal that lives in Mexico and the southwestern United States. The bats weigh only about one ounce (28 g) and are approximately 3 inches (7.5 cm) long. However, these bats have a wingspan measuring 10 inches (25 cm). As its name suggests, the lesser long-nosed bat has a long, narrow nose. Its tongue is also long, with a tip like a brush that it uses to drink **nectar** from flowers. The bats live mainly in areas of **thornscrub**, deciduous forests, and the Sonoran Desert in Arizona. They make their **roosts** in caves, rocks, and abandoned mines. Thousands of bats can live in one roost, although males sometimes roost alone. By the late 1980s, **culling**, or killing, roost disturbance, and **habitat** destruction had reduced the population to around 1,000 individuals.

Lesser long-nosed bats are nocturnal and feed at night. They hover over cactus and agave blooms and drink the nectar with their long tongues. These bats can live for up to 20 years if they are left alone.

LESSER LONG-NOSED BAT FACTS

Lesser long-nosed bats feed on **pollen** and nectar. They get all the nutrients they need from the flowers of blue agave plants and the Saguaro and Organ Pipe cacti. These plants grow along the **migration** route of the lesser long-nosed bat. This route is known as the nectar trail, and it is important for the bats on their long, yearly journey between Mexico and the Sonoran Desert. With their long wings, the bats can fly at approximately 14 miles (22.5 km) an hour. They also use their wings to hover next to the flowers while they feed. Lesser long-nosed bats are nocturnal, which means they are active at night. They live in large groups called **colonies**. Every year, the bats fly thousands of miles north to Arizona to feed on cactus flowers. Females give birth to a single **pup** in damp caves called **maternity roosts**. The bats return to Mexico when the pups are strong enough to make the long journey.

Tucson Mountain Park in Arizona's Sonoran Desert. Lesser long-nosed bats feed on Saguaro and Organ Pipe cacti. Scientists work to protect desert habitats for bats.

Species at Risk

Created in 1984, the International Union for the **Conservation** of Nature (IUCN) protects wildlife, plants, and **natural resources** around the world. Its members include about 1,400 governments and nongovernmental organizations. The IUCN publishes the Red List of Threatened Species each year, which tells people how likely a plant or animal species is to become **extinct**. It began publishing the list in 1964.

The Pinta giant tortoise lived on one of the Galapagos Islands. It was last assessed by the IUCN in 2015, and is now classed as Extinct (EX). The IUCN updates the Red List twice a year to track the changing of species. Each individual species is reevaluated at least every five years.

SCIENTIFIC CRITERIA

The Red List, created by scientists, divides nearly 80,000 species of plants and animals into nine categories. Criteria for each category include the growth and **decline** of the population size of a species. They also include how many individuals within a species can breed, or have babies. In addition, scientists include information about the habitat of the species, such as its size and quality. These criteria allow scientists to figure out the probability of extinction facing the species.

IUCN LEVELS OF THREAT

The Red List uses nine categories to define the threat to a species.

Extinct (EX)	No living individuals survive
Extinct in the Wild (EW)	Species cannot be found in its natural habitat. Exists only in **captivity**, in **cultivation**, or in an area that is not its natural habitat
Critically Endangered (CR)	At extremely high risk of becoming extinct in the wild
Endangered (EN)	At very high risk of extinction in the wild
Vulnerable (VU)	At high risk of extinction in the wild
Near Threatened (NT)	Likely to become threatened in the near future
Least Concern (LC)	Widespread, abundant, or at low risk
Data Deficient (DD)	Not enough data to make a judgment about the species
Not Evaluated (NE)	Not yet evaluated against the criteria

In the United States, the Endangered Species Act of 1973 was passed to protect species from possible extinction. It has its own criteria for classifying species, but they are similar to those of the IUCN. Canada introduced the Species at Risk Act in 2002. More than 530 species are protected under the act. The list of species is compiled by the Committee on the Status of Endangered Wildlife in Canada (COSEWIC).

BATS AT RISK

In the 1980s, less than 1,000 lesser long-nosed bats were found in a total of 14 roosts. The IUCN Red List classified them as Vulnerable (VU) in 2008. In 2015, they were downgraded to Near Threatened (NT). Recent figures show the population has risen to around 200,000, with the number of roosts rising to 75. In 2018, this species was the first bat in North America to be removed from the Endangered Species Act.

The Human Threat

One of the greatest threats faced by lesser long-nosed bats was from humans. Some species of bats carry disease and many people were afraid of them. In Mexico, vampire bats were a problem for farmers because these bats carry a disease called **rabies**. Vampire bats bite and infect cattle, which die. As a result, farmers killed vampire bats. Farmers damaged roosting caves using fire, gas, and dynamite. In some places, entrances to caves were sealed. Even though lesser long-nosed bats do not carry rabies, they were killed in huge numbers because people could not tell the difference between the bat species. Construction of settlements along the nectar trail also damaged or destroyed the habitat for the migrating lesser long-nosed bats.

Three species of vampire bats feed on blood. They are native to North, Central, and South America, and are most common in Mexico, Brazil, Chile, and Argentina. Farmers trying to protect their cattle killed lesser long-nosed bats along with the vampire bats.

AGAVE POLLINATION

Agave plants only produce flowers once in their life. After that, the plants die. It can take seven years for a plant to bloom, so it is a long, slow process. Just before flowering, agaves grow a tall **stalk**. At that time, agaves contain the most sugar. For many years, farmers harvested agave plants before they flowered. They used the sugar to make a drink called **tequila**. As tequila became popular, more agave plants were harvested. This created a problem. Without agave flowers, lesser long-nosed bats lost an important food source. That loss also had a negative impact on agave plants. When the bats flew from plant to plant, they pollinated agaves, resulting in the growth of healthy new plants.

Balancing the Ecosystem

The Saguaro cactus blooms at night. Its white flowers produce a scent that smells like melon. This attracts lesser long-nosed bats. They use their long **snouts** to reach into the flowers for nectar. Pollen sticks to their hairy faces, and as the bats fly among the cacti, it falls off into other flowers, pollinating them. Lesser long-nosed bats keep the **ecosystem** healthy by spreading pollen so that new cacti can grow. This helps other species to flourish. White-tailed deer feed on Saguaro stalks, and the cacti are used by red-tailed hawks as perches. The plants can grow up to 50 feet (15 m) tall, so they make safe places for birds to build their nests well out of the reach of **predators**.

Birds such as elf owls, woodpeckers (right), and white-winged doves make their nests in the crevices of the Saguaro cacti. The birds help to spread seeds from the fruit through their waste.

CLOSE RELATIONSHIPS

In the summer, lesser long-nosed bats eat the red Saguaro fruit when it ripens. Seeds from the fruit pass through into the soil in bat waste and grow into new Saguaro plants. The waste also helps to keep the soil healthy. This kind of relationship is called **symbiotic**. If the plant or bat was removed from the ecosystem, the other would have difficulty surviving. This relationship also applies to the agave plant. The agave blooms at night, when bats are active. Agave is important food along the migration route from Mexico to the Sonoran Desert. The bats migrate at the same time of year as agave flowers bloom. In the years when the bat population was very low, scientists noticed that agave plants produced far fewer seeds than normal.

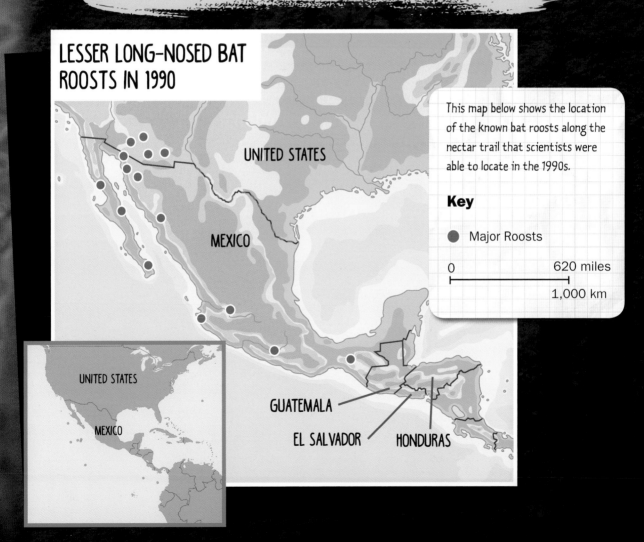

LESSER LONG-NOSED BAT ROOSTS IN 1990

UNITED STATES

MEXICO

This map below shows the location of the known bat roosts along the nectar trail that scientists were able to locate in the 1990s.

Key

● Major Roosts

0   620 miles

1,000 km

UNITED STATES

MEXICO

GUATEMALA

EL SALVADOR

HONDURAS

Disappearing Food Source

Agave plants do not need pollination to reproduce. Each plant can grow into a new plant from shoots at the base of its stem. However, these agaves are **clones**. They are exactly the same as the plant they grew from. This means they are not healthy enough to survive pests and diseases. In the late 1990s, a disease killed 25 percent of the agave plants in Mexico. About 40 percent of agave crops are still affected by disease, but plants that grow from pollination are healthier. When some farmers lost their entire crop of cloned agaves, they realized that change was needed. A group called the Tequila Interchange Project worked with the farmers. They introduced new farming methods that helped them to grow healthier crops, which also helped the lesser long-nosed bat population.

Many people in Mexico depend on agave plants to make a living. They use the dried fibers in the manufacture of carpets, paper, fiberglass, and other items, such as baskets, belts, and hats. The sap is used to make natural sweeteners.

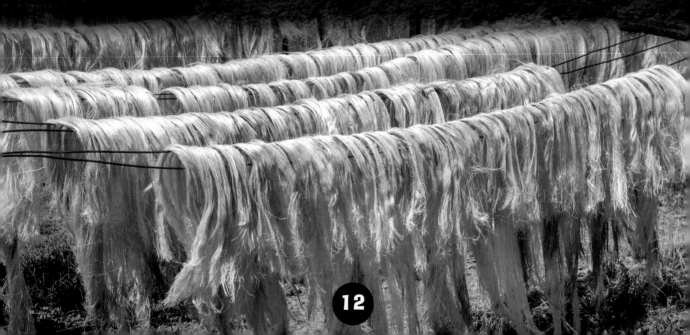

Blue agave plants that reproduce from shoots, rather than from pollination by lesser long-nosed bats, suffer from more diseases. They are also more likely to be attacked by pests such as the Giant Agave Bug. This insect pierces the bud or fruit of the flower and sucks out the liquid.

COLLABORATING FOR A CAUSE

Bat Conservation International (BCI) was founded in 1982 to protect all bats and their ecosystems around the world. They partnered with government organizations and private groups to help the lesser long-nosed bat. They focused on saving habitats and preventing the destruction of roosts. Many other people joined the struggle to save the lesser long-nosed bat. In 2006, Scott Richardson, right, a wildlife **biologist** from Tucson, Arizona, began a local program called Citizen Scientists. The group of **volunteers** helped researchers by **monitoring** the bats in their own backyards. Government groups in the United States and Mexico also worked as partners: the U.S. Forest Service, National Park Service, U.S. Fish and Wildlife Service, U.S. Army's Fort Huachuca, and the Government of Mexico.

An Action Plan

Two and a half acres (1 ha), or roughly the area of about two football fields, of agave is enough to feed 100 lesser long-nosed bats for one night. To improve habitats, more agave was planted in the wild and left to bloom naturally for bats to pollinate. **Conservationists** put plans in place to protect the bats' feeding grounds and roosts. Researchers located roosts in caves and abandoned mine shafts, and looked at ways they might discourage people from entering, damaging, or destroying them. In the early 2000s, the BCI, Arizona-Sonora Desert Museum, and conservationists in Mexico City began an education program aimed at informing people about the importance of the lesser long-nosed bat for the survival of the ecosystem and its many animals, birds, plants, and insects.

Lesser long-nosed bats roost during the day in colonies that can number up to several thousand individuals. Planting more agave plants was an important step in increasing bat populations.

Lesser long-nosed bats spend the winter in caves in Mexico. They migrate north in the spring and summer. When they are not out looking for food at night, they rest in their roosts. Protecting the roosts was an important part of the action plan.

MONITORING THE BATS

It was a difficult task counting and monitoring lesser long-nosed bats because they were mainly active at night. Their preferred roosting areas were located away from people. Researchers realized that if they could monitor bat movements they would have a better understanding of when the bats were traveling. They would also know how many bats were passing through an area at the same time. As new technologies developed, more accurate ways of monitoring the bats were used. Bat detectors convert the **echolocation** signals from bats into audible clicks and pops. These can then be analyzed by scientists.

Making the Plan Work

In 1988, when the lesser long-nosed bat was listed as an endangered species in the United States and Mexico, federal agencies controlled most of the areas where the bats roosted and fed. In 1997, the U.S. Forest Service, National Parks Service, and Fort Huachuca created a recovery plan for the bats that involved planting blue agave, Saguaro cacti, and Organ Pipe cacti on their land. The plants were expected to increase through pollination. The habitat would sustain itself. Plants would be left to grow without being harvested by farmers before they could flower. Organizations also worked together to protect the roosts. BCI, the National Park Service, USFWS, and wildlife and conservation organizations worked to design, fund, and install bat gates.

Part of the federal recovery plan was to encourage wild agave and cacti to grow without human interference. This would also help the bat population to increase.

BAT GATES

The best way to protect roosts is to stop people from entering caves and disused mine shafts. Gates are an ideal way to do this. They do not affect the airflow, temperature, and humidity inside the roost. Most bat gates have several steel bars placed horizontally across the roost entrance. These gates prevent predators, including people, from entering but bats can pass through them easily. Video cameras were installed at some disused mines. Researchers wanted to see whether the gates had any negative effects on the bats. A scientific study in June 2018 found that the bats became used to the gates very quickly and suffered no injuries flying in and out. The video cameras also enabled researchers to count the number of bats using the mines.

Bat-Friendly Farming

In 2014, the Tequila Interchange Project and Rodrigo Medellin, an ecology professor at the University of Mexico, persuaded farmers to change the way they were harvesting agave. Farmers agreed to leave five percent of every 2.5 acres (1 ha) of agave they grew so that it could flower and be pollinated by lesser long-nosed bats. The remaining 95 percent of their crop could still be harvested before it flowered, when the plants contained the most sugar. This was called bat-friendly farming, and tequila producers using this method were allowed to have a special "bat-friendly tequila" label on their bottles. Farmers also began to plant agaves in rocky areas or at the edges of their properties. These were also left for the bats to pollinate.

To make tequila, farmers cut away the leaves of the agave plant before it grows a stalk and flowers. The core that is left is baked, then pulped to extract the juice.

COLLABORATING FOR A CAUSE

Rodrigo Medellin is known as the "Bat Man" because of his work. He has played a major role in saving the lesser long-nosed bats. After working to have them listed under the Endangered Species Act in the 1980s, Medellin helped to establish safe roosts. While researching the nectar trail, he met with agave farmers in Mexico. He explained the advantages of leaving part of their crops for the bats. When the farmers failed to take notice, Medellin went back to talk to them again. Years later, after a poor agave harvest, they realized that the bats were helping to produce healthier crops. They finally agreed to try his ideas.

Five percent of the agave crop produces long stems and flowers. Lesser long-nosed bats have a source of food. The farmers have the benefit of a stronger, naturally pollinated crop in years to come.

Saving the Species

Technology was an effective part of conservation efforts. Infrared cameras were used to film bats. Some bats were fitted with radio transmitters. These methods helped researchers to count bats more accurately. The information also helped to locate roosts, which could then be monitored and protected. Many local people became enthusiastic "citizen scientists." Some organized bat-watching parties. People interested in flowers were also involved. They recorded the times when they observed lesser long-nosed bats feeding from Saguaro and Organ Pipe cacti and blue agaves.

When lesser long-nosed bats push their noses into cacti to drink the nectar, pollen sticks to their faces. These bats in a roost in Mexico have just returned from feeding on cacti. Their faces are covered with pollen.

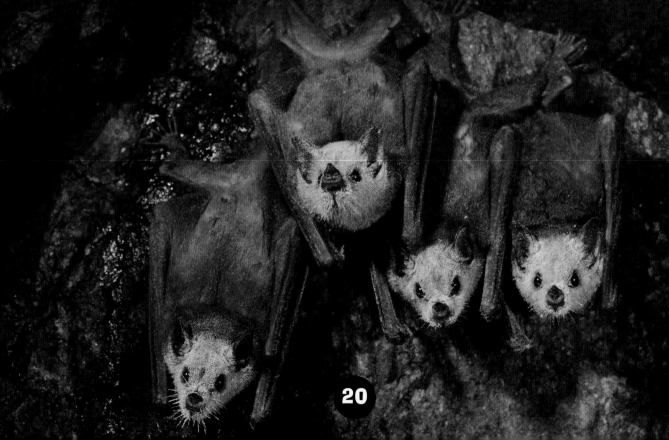

COLLABORATING FOR A CAUSE

Over 10 years, about 140 residents of Tucson, Arizona, worked with the U.S. Fish and Wildlife Service to track lesser long-nosed bats as they migrated through their neighborhoods. In 2007, the local people involved in this project became known as Citizen Scientists. Many noticed that hummingbird feeders in their yards were empty each morning. This was unusual, because hummingbirds are active during the day, not the night. The agave crop had failed that year and bats had to find another source of food along the nectar trail. They were drinking the sugar water from the hummingbird feeders. More people began to put hummingbird feeders in their yards. They filled them with sugary water, then waited for the bats. When the bats arrived, they made a note of the date and the time. Biologists set up nets nearby so they could catch the bats for observation. When bats flew into the nets, a detector went off. Biologists, helped by the local citizens, weighed and measured the bats before releasing them to continue on their migration.

Education Campaigns

The IUCN has an international education program for bat conservation. In Mexico, bat biologists used stories, games, and a mascot called Marcelo to teach children about bats and how to identify them. The sessions were fun and informative, resulting in many children sharing with their families what they had been taught. When the children were given true and false quizzes, the results showed that they had engaged fully with the information they had been given. This was a successful project. It changed people's views about bats, helped them to identify them correctly, and put an end to some of the fears that people had previously had about them.

Marcelo, the Mexican bat mascot, was used as part of an education program. Between April 2011 and March 2014, Marcelo traveled through Latin America. Children in each country visited by Marcelo wrote a short essay about bats. These were collected in a notebook. The project inspired similar projects in other countries around the world.

POPULATION RECOVERY

In Mexico, **binational** education programs to change agave farming methods and the way people thought about bats began to make a difference. Between 1990 and 2010, lesser long-nosed bats were found in more than 40 percent of the country. Mexico **delisted** lesser long-nosed bats from the Endangered Species Act in 2015. Their **range** still spreads from southern Mexico to the states of Arizona and New Mexico, but their population is much higher than it was in the 1980s, when the bats faced extinction in the wild.

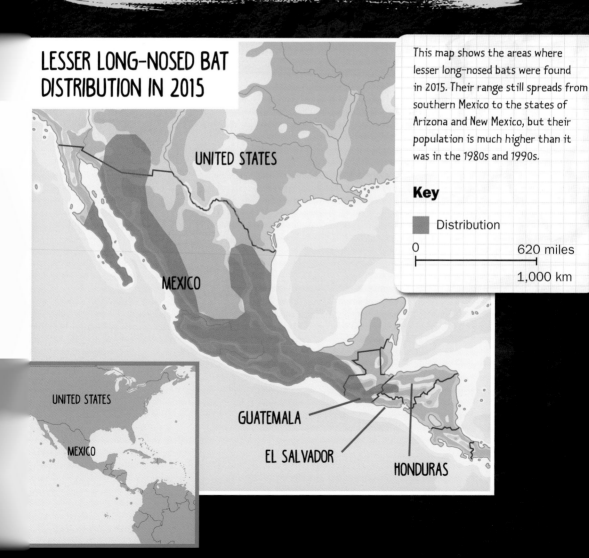

LESSER LONG-NOSED BAT DISTRIBUTION IN 2015

This map shows the areas where lesser long-nosed bats were found in 2015. Their range still spreads from southern Mexico to the states of Arizona and New Mexico, but their population is much higher than it was in the 1980s and 1990s.

Key

Distribution

0   620 miles

1,000 km

UNITED STATES

MEXICO

GUATEMALA

EL SALVADOR

HONDURAS

UNITED STATES

MEXICO

Looking to the Future

When the lesser long-nosed bat was removed from the Endangered Species list in the United States, it no longer qualified for the same amount of funding to help protect its roosts and habitat. However, the post-delisting monitoring program recommended that roosts with more than 1,000 bats should continue to be monitored for five years. Volunteers and researchers will continue to count bat populations and monitor the nectar trail. This will warn researchers if the bat population starts to decline again, or if new threats to the roosts appear. Monitoring will also reveal if climate changes are affecting food plants. If agave on the nectar trail fails to bloom at the same time as the bat migration, this will cause problems. Fortunately, federal agencies manage the land where the bats roost. They can control how people use the land, and have powers to stop or limit activities such as off-roading. There are also now laws in place to protect caves and bats from being harmed in any way. There are strict penalties for anyone who breaks the law.

Merlin Tuttle is a conservationist and wildlife photographer. He specializes in bats. He founded BCI and Merlin Tuttle's Bat Conservation. These two organizations continue to protect and collect data on the lesser long-nosed bat.

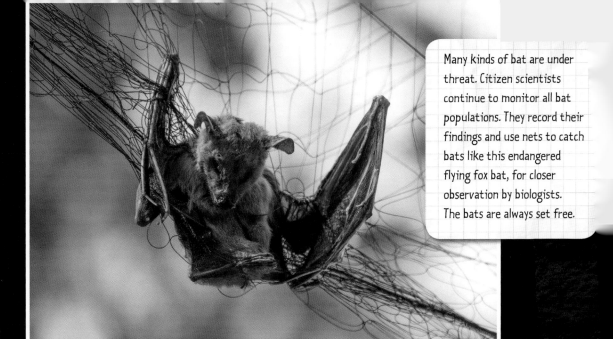

Many kinds of bat are under threat. Citizen scientists continue to monitor all bat populations. They record their findings and use nets to catch bats like this endangered flying fox bat, for closer observation by biologists. The bats are always set free.

BAT CAVE TOURS

Lesser long-nosed bats only give birth to one pup each year. The humid caves of the maternity roosts are the best environment for the health of mothers and pups. However, when people visit caves, this changes the cave's humidity. As people have become increasingly interested in bats, they want to see them for themselves. Some landowners organize cave tours where people can observe bat species, including the lesser long-nosed bat. Most people now understand why bats are important to the ecosystem. This knowledge helps landowners to limit or prevent people from touring or visiting caves if they think this could be a threat to the bats.

Saving Other Bat Species

BCI reports that there are 47 species of bats in the United States and Canada. This is about 3 percent of the global bat population. Lessons learned in the recovery plan for the lesser long-nosed bat are being used to help protect the roosts and habitats of other bat species. But there are other, new threats. Some bats are affected by a disease called white-nose syndrome, which causes them to wake more often than normal during **hibernation**. The disease has already killed millions of bats. Wind turbines pose another threat. BCI estimates that about 200,000 bats are killed every year when they fly into turbine blades.

FLORIDA BONNETED BAT

This is the rarest bat species in the United States and is now found in only a few areas of Florida. The bats live in small groups, roosting in chimneys and attics, hollowed-out trees, and sometimes under rocks. It is thought that fewer than 1,000 of these bats still exist. Threats to their survival include the use of pesticides, logging, and extreme weather such as storms and flooding. The IUCN classifies their status as Vulnerable (VU).

THE GREATER LONG-NOSED BAT

The greater long-nosed bat lives in Mexico and a small area of the southern U.S. It shares some of the challenges to its survival with the lesser long-nosed bat. Both suffered from their roosts being

disturbed or destroyed, as well as by the loss of their main food source. The IUCN now classes the greater long-nosed bat as being Endangered (EN), with its population still falling. IUCN estimates say the bat's numbers may have fallen by more than 50 percent in the last 30 years. Bat organizations are looking to use their experience with the lesser long-nosed bat to save this species from extinction.

THE LITTLE BROWN BAT

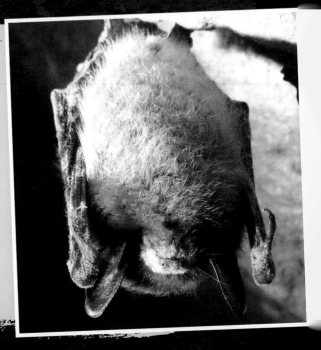

This bat lives in Canada and the United States. It was last assessed by the IUCN in 2018, when it was classed as Endangered (EN). The population of little brown bats has been severely affected by the spread of white-nose syndrome (see right). Other threats are loss of habitat and the negative effects of wind turbines. IUCN predictions are that the population of little brown bats will continue to fall.

What Can You Do to Help?

The lesser long-nosed bat is back from the brink of extinction, but it is far from safe. Saving bats takes commitment from everyone. A great way to get involved is to build or buy a bat house and put it in your backyard. The bats will also help to pollinate the flowers in the neighborhood. The BCI website has lots of information on bat houses and how to attract bats to your backyard, as well as how to become more involved in saving bats.

There are many different kinds of bat houses that you can buy. Make sure the one you buy has Bat Approved Certification. You can attach bat houses to trees or poles, but bats prefer to use bat houses that are hung high up on the sides of buildings or wooden sheds.

Keeping the environment healthy is good for bats and humans. Join a clean-up group to pick up garbage and tidy up woodlands and green spaces.

LEAVE BATS ALONE!

If you hike or camp in areas where bats roost, be bat-aware when going into caves. Be sure to obey any signs telling you to keep out. There are also some things you can do to help bats:

- Find out if you live in an area where bat research is needed, and become a Citizen Scientist like the residents of Tucson. Contact conservation groups in your state to find out if there are other ways you can be involved in observing bat behavior.

- Did you know that Bat Week happens every October? Conservation organizations and government groups in the U.S. and Canada partner to make people more aware of bats. Find out what activities are happening near you, and get your school involved in some of them.

- Contact your local elected officials to tell them that wildlife and habitat protection are important to your future. Make the case for the continued protection of bats that are still endangered.

Learning More

Books

Mara, Wil. *Bats* (Backyard Safari). Cavendish Square, 2014.

Markle, Sandra. *The Case of the Vanishing Little Brown Bats: A Scientific Mystery*. Millbrook Press, 2014.

Niver, Heather Moore. *Vampire Bats After Dark* (Animals of the Night). Enslow Publishing, 2016.

Samuelson, Benjamin O. *Journey of the Bats* (Massive Animal Migrations). Gareth Stevens Publishing, 2018.

On the Web

www.nationalgeographic.com/
animals/2018/10/animals-
endangered-back-from-brink-
conservation-news/
Information on the lesser long-nosed bat from the National Geographic website, including a video of the bat flying in slow motion.

www.batcon.org/resources/media-
education/learning/bat-squad
Pages from BCI featuring the Bat Squad! webcast series showing how to be a bat conservationist in your own backyard.

www.youtube.com/
watch?v=dmVZAMHO3Cg
Watch this video for easy-to-follow instructions to make a cute origami bat!

www.nps.gov/subjects/bats/myth-
busters.htm
The National Park Service website debunks popular myths about bats.

For videos, activities, and more, enter the access code at the Crabtree Plus website below.

www.crabtreeplus.com/animals-back-brink

Access code: abb37

Glossary

binational Involving two countries

biologist A scientist who studies living organisms

clone An organism that is exactly the same as the one from which it was produced

colonies Groups of bats

conservation The careful use of resources

conservationists People who work to protect plants, animals, and natural resources

culling Reducing the population of wild animals by killing them

cultivation Preparation of land to grow plants or crops

decline Decrease

delisted When something has been removed from a list

echolocation Working out the location of something by measuring the time it takes for an echo to return from it

ecosystem All living things in a particular area and how they interact

extinct When all the members of a species have died

habitat The conditions in which an animal or plant naturally lives

hibernation The state of resting or deep sleep that some animals go into to save their energy, usually in winter

maternity roosts Places where females gather together to give birth and to feed their young

migration The seasonal movement of animals or birds to another region

monitoring Observing something closely

natural resources Materials from nature that are useful

nectar The sweet, sugary liquid made by plants

pollen A fine powder produced by plants

predators Any animals that live by killing and eating other animals

pup Young and newborn bats

rabies An infectious disease spread by animal bites

range The geographical area in which an animal usually lives

roosts The places where bats settle together during the day

snouts Long, narrow noses

stalk The stem of a plant

symbiotic A relationship that equally benefits two living organisms

tequila A Mexican alcoholic drink made from agave plants

thornscrub An area of small trees, shrubs, and cacti

volunteers People who work without getting paid

Index and About the Author

ABOUT THE AUTHOR
Ruth Daly has more than 25 years of teaching experience, mainly in elementary schools, and she currently teaches Grade 3. She has written more than 45 nonfiction books for the education market on a wide range of subjects and for a variety of age groups. These include books on animals, life cycles, and the natural environment. Her fiction and poetry have been published in magazines and literary journals. She enjoys travel, reading, and photography, particularly of nature and wildlife.